SONDER

Spiritual Fiction

NANIMA SERIES
BOOK III

DONNA GODDARD

CONTENTS

PROLOGUE
DAWNING REALISATION

Sonder is the realisation that everyone has a story, and, for some people, you are merely a random passerby, an extra sipping coffee in the background.—The Dictionary of Obscure Sorrows by John Koenig

The increasing realisation that
every life and life form is as
intricate and marvellous as our own
is an indication of developing consciousness.

PART I
SOLSTICE
SUMMER

QI IS IN ME

CHAPTER 1

FIERY FATHER

December 22nd:

It was summer solstice and a few days before Christmas. The sun was at its highest, and the days were at their longest. The southern face of Earth was directly turned towards its source of power and light—its fiery father. The summer solstice is a time of maleness, a time for masculine qualities, which we should all have a balance of. It's a time for looking outward, being outside, speaking up, and generally doing stuff.

Being nestled in the ranges, the summer temperatures of Black Forest were considerably less than the lowlands. It was Maliyan's first summer in Black Forest, but she had already learned not to wrap summer in the concept of heat—instead to see it in terms of long days of light, relatively less clothing, and usually (but not always) unnecessary heating. It was a milder notion of summer. It meant you could go for an evening walk. It was a break from the long cold rather than a powerful hot season in its own right.

As Maliyan passed *Sonder,* the most popular cafe in

town, she heard a woman say, "It's so beautiful out here that I would move too, but an eigth-month winter is too long for me."

"Nonsense. Who told you that? Winter isn't eight months," said her male friend with a smile. "It's more like ten. And the other two, your house can burn down!"

Living next to a forest, everyone had to be fire-aware.

Someone had humorously decorated a large weed growing tenaciously through a crack of the dilapidated Municipal Council building next to Sonder. The baubles and tinsel merely drew attention to the building's unkempt state.

A woman descended the railway steps and clattered along the footpath with her suitcase. She probably caught the train out from the city to stay with her parents over the Christmas break. Her high heels were impractical for travelling. No doubt, she preferred city living to country comfort.

Maliyan walked through the miniature Christmas trees individually decorated by the local businesses. A sweet one had a hidden alcove amongst the branches with a tiny community of fairies and birds. All the businesses contributed, but there was a big discrepancy in tree-decorating talent. The worst one consisted of gum tree branches, which looked good for two days and then became a brown, dried-out structure of lifeless garden rubbish. A lone, silver tinsel star sat at the top, heavily leaning to one side. It didn't have a business name attached.

The unofficial but unanimous winner was an earthworks company that made a bright, sparkly tree with yellow toy trucks circling it, filled with red, green, and gold

Christmas baubles. "Surprised they are still there," visitors would say as they pointed to the toy trucks. Not only did toy trucks stay in their rightful place, but cafe tables and chairs were left out overnight and were still there every morning. Safe to say, the crime rate was low.

CHAPTER 2

JIHUI AND ROBERT

Turning left, Maliyan stopped at a cottage in a side street. An A-board was placed on the sidewalk, saying:

FREE
Summer Solstice Empowerment
QiGong*
All welcome

A man at the entrance of the open shed smiled calmly and warmly. He gestured for Maliyan to come closer.

Bowing, he said, "My name is Robert. My Chinese name is Jihui." Seeing that Maliyan was engaged, he continued, "When my wife and I first came to Australia, the immigration officer asked me if I had an English name.

---

* Qi (pronounced che) means life force. QiGong is a traditional Taoist Chinese mind-body practice combining movement, breath, and meditation to improve balance, flexibility, strength, health, and energetic well-being.

I had forgotten to pick one, and Robert was the first name that popped into my mind. So, Robert, it has remained."

He laughed quietly, and his eyes sparkled. His face was lineless, making it hard to tell how old he was, but his demeanour had the wisdom of age.

"Would you like to join us for qigong summer solstice empowerment?" asked Robert. "It's free—the session, summer solstice, and empowerment."

Entering the little shed, Maliyan sat on the floor with eight other people, all Chinese. She had a Chinese strain of DNA in her. Along with white settlers, they were the first non-Aboriginal people to come to Nanima. As a result, many Nanima families had some Chinese in them, although it was typically not acknowledged. She knew nothing about her paternal Chinese relative. A hairdresser once told Maliyan that she had Chinese hair because it sat so firmly in the direction it wanted to go. A local of Black Forest told Maliyan that her profile was identical to Penny Wong (a well-known Chinese-Australian politician). Wong was the first Asian Australian in Cabinet and the first openly lesbian federal parliamentarian in Australia.

"I hope you don't mind," he added tentatively.

"Of course not," said Maliyan. "She's one of the few politicians we trust, and she's a powerhouse."

CHAPTER 3

MR TANNER AND
MASTER XIAO

"As we have some new people," said Robert [Maliyan was fairly sure that she was the only new person], "I will tell you a little of my story."

"I met my master, Master Xiao, when I was an eight-year-old boy in the early years of the Chinese Cultural Revolution, which began in 1966 and lasted for a disastrous decade."

Robert must be around sixty, thought Maliyan.

"Neither I, my family, nor the residents of our town knew that Master Xiao was a highly accomplished martial artist and qigong healer. We simply knew him as Mr Tanner, a gentle, quiet man who recently started working in the lowly job of boiler room attendant across the road from where we lived. I was sick with a mysterious illness that prevented me from attending school. When my parents were at work, I snuck out of the house out of boredom and began investigating everything I could get into. I soon came across the boiler room, and something about Mr Tanner's laughing eyes drew me into that hot space. I began calling in every day, and Mr Tanner asked me if I would like to learn martial arts from him. Of course, I said yes. However, I had to keep it a secret for everyone's safety.

I barely noticed that my health issue quickly disappeared. My training from Mr Tanner went on for many years. Eventually, my parents had to know. Along with my martial arts training, I began developing qigong energy abilities. After seven intense and marvellous years, a great shock came to me. The Cultural Revolution ended, and Mr Tanner had to return to the Buddhist monastery high in the remote mountains he came from. Mr Tanner was, in fact, Master Xiao, a widely respected and extraordinary monk at the temple. The monastery had been disbanded at the beginning of the Cultural Revolution, and all the monks had to return to their families. As Master Xiao was an orphan, he had no family to return to. Thus, he roamed the countryside for a few years before settling across the road from me.

After Master Xiao returned to his beloved Buddhist community, I continued my training with him. That meant many hours of travel during the school holidays by train and bus and then a five-hour trek up the mountain. My master did not want me to become a monk. He wanted me to be educated and travel to the West with the lineage."

Robert paused, looked at the clock, and said, "So, here I am. Let's begin."

After the summer solstice empowerment, which consisted of various qigong exercises, Robert said that they were going to see Master Xiao tomorrow, and everyone was welcome to attend.

CHAPTER 4

MEETING A MASTER

The next day:

It was an hour's drive to the mountain and then a two-hour trek to the top. Master Xiao was on an extended stay from China to celebrate his 94th birthday and would soon return to his own mountain. Maliyan decided to go with them because how often do you get to meet a master?

The mountain track was steep. Everyone seemed to be fitter than Maliyan. Maybe they were used to coming here to see Master Xiao. The little group stopped every half hour. If they were stopping for her, they didn't make it obvious. They said they were having a nature break, meditation break, or looking-at-the-view break.

Robert patiently walked beside her. He was an engaging storyteller and made the uphill trek considerably less tiring than it otherwise would have been. Along the way, she learned much about him, the master, and qigong. Maliyan concluded that underneath Robert's humble, relaxed, and unassuming manner was a powerful mind and significant spiritual accomplishment.

CHAPTER 5

SIX SOUNDS

The view from the top was spectacular. The simple temple and surrounding buildings took nothing from the mountain's glory. Everything seemed to be there to serve the cause of life in its magnificent, unadulterated beauty.

Master Xiao embodied effervescent happiness, peace, and ease. He was unexpectedly slight, given his still active physical abilities. Robert told Maliyan that when he first met his master, he was surprised that such a modest body could perform the feats that it did. He found it very amusing that if they walked in an unsafe area at night, his master's unimpressive build would appear as easy prey for robbers. He laughed heartily and said, "That was a grave mistake!"

As Master Xiao couldn't speak English, Robert translated the session.

"During the sixth century," said Master Xiao, "a QiGong master, who was nicknamed *Grand Councillor of the Mountains,* identified six sounds that have a unique healing effect on the human body. Each corresponds to a specific organ and energy system. Today, we will practise them."

The master explained the sounds, the relevant organs, and the order in which they would be chanted. They were:

1. Xu (pronounced shee) for liver
2. He (pronounced huh) for heart
3. Hu (pronounced hoo) for spleen
4. Si (pronounced suh) for lungs
5. Chui (pronounced chway) for kidneys
6. Xi (pronounced see) for the three centres or dantians

"The three dantians," said Master Xiao, "are the centres of qi or life force in our body."

The process was slowly taught over several hours. Then everyone ate a simple lunch. After that, the six healing sounds were practised reverently and profoundly. One of Maliyan's favourite bits was whenever Master Xiao said in Chinese, "I am in Qi. Qi is in me." There was something about how he said the words that radiated a powerful energy transfer. The words bristled with intensity and brightness.

At the end of the day, Master Xiao said,

"Many of the most magnificent things in our world happen gently, graciously, and with no fanfare—the movement of the sun, the stars, the moon, the ocean, and the constant miracles of creation in the natural world. You, too, can become a force of nature. Don't be afraid that your growth has to be painful and dramatic, involving lots of outward change. More often than not, it is a gentle unfolding of what is beautiful, true, purposeful and serene."

I am in Qi. Qi is in me.

PART II
LIVING IN FOG
WINTER

EVERYONE HAS A STORY

CHAPTER 6

AN EXTRA IN THE BACKGROUND

Six months later, in late June:

When the first month of winter is as cold as Black Forest, the long stretch ahead can seem rather daunting. The outside section of Sonder was empty, although inside was busy and buzzing as usual. The other cafes in town did alright, enough to get by, with the bonus of freedom. They would shut for all sorts of reasons—fire weather, winter break, baby born, spouse sick, no staff, mental health, changed our minds. Sonder, however, was different. The owners had run a thriving inner-city cafe and brought all their vibe and work ethic out to Black Forest when they decided on a lifestyle change for their young family. The couple were always pleasant to customers but a little reserved. Their focus was on running the business.

One day, Maliyan said to Ronny, one of the owners, "Did you name your cafe after the invented word?"

Ronny looked at her half-surprised, half-suspicious and said, "You know what it means?"

He waited for validation that she really did know the meaning of sonder.

"Ahh, something about…" said Maliyan, scrambling for a passable definition, "other people's lives being are as complex and real as our own."

"Yes," said Ronny, satisfied with her response. "Everyone has a story and, for some people, we are merely a random passerby, an extra sipping coffee in the background."

After a pause, he added, "You are only the second person to come in here who knows what the word means."

"Maybe others have known but didn't bother to say," said Maliyan.

Ronny's face suggested that he doubted that. From that moment on, they were friends.

CHAPTER 7

PASSERSBY

Luna pulled his beanie lower as he surveyed Sonder's vacant outdoor area. He had learned that when he drove out to Black Forest, he needed extra layers.

"Grand German shepherd," said a passerby, pointing to Iggy.

"Bit chilly," said Luna.

"Ahh, don't you mind that," said the man. "It's the cold and low-lying cloud (the dome, as we call it) that keeps them city folk from moving out here."

Luna tried to look less citified. He saw on his phone that it was winter solstice. It was a year since his first trip to Black Forest and six months since his move this way. As it turned out, he was living and working in the city and travelling the hour to Black Forest about once a month.

Maliyan kissed Luna hello, patted Iggy, and sat down.

A talkative couple exited Sonder and said, "Well-behaved dog. No lead. No nothing. No coat? You've got one."

"German shepherds have double coats," said Luna. "He's already got his winter coat on, and it's perfectly coordinated with his colouring."

CHAPTER 8

DOZEN A DAY

"Weak latte, I assume?" said Luna.

"No," said Maliyan, "I'm off caffeine. A few days after I saw you last, my body told me to get decaffeinated coffee in the mornings. So, I did. And a couple of days after that, it told me to get rid of the real drug."

"What drug?" asked Luna.

"Tea," said Maliyan. "One weak coffee a day was nothing compared to my tea intake. Country women of my generation are big tea drinkers. My sisters, female cousins, and I were all drinking tea by the time we were twelve. Lots of it. I probably drink a dozen cups of tea a day. Anyway, my body told me to drink decaffeinated tea instead."

"How did that go?" asked Luna.

"For a few days, I was falling asleep, and I felt depressed for no apparent reason. But then, my nervous system and whole digestive system got on board and started working much better than before."

Luna frowned and said, "It's *not* a real drug."

CHAPTER 9

SHROUDED IN MIST

"Except for a few short breaks," continued Luna with averted eyes, "I've always been a big weed user. Not public. It's been a private thing, which is probably worse."

Although Maliyan didn't know this about Luna, she was not surprised. A person of his sensitivities has to find some way of coping with life.

"You weren't using it when I was living in the shop-house a year and a half ago," said Maliyan.

"That was one of the short breaks," said Luna. "It's also why I deteriorated as the time went on. I wasn't ready to give it up." He looked uncomfortable but rallied himself and said, "When I moved down here, I knew that if I didn't get off it, I was going to create the same life all over again. And I wanted something better." Turning to the nearby mountain of Geboor, he could see that its summit was shrouded in mist. "So, yeah, I've been off it for six months. It's been really tough. It has affected me in many ways—eating, sleeping, what I do with my time. The worst side effects have been inability to sleep and brain fog. Thankfully, the fog is lifting now."

"So you decided to tell me," said Maliyan.

"Yeah," said Luna.

Maliyan leaned over the table, put her hand on Luna's shoulder, and said, "I've never been prouder of you."

THE LESSENING

CHAPTER 10

LONGTIME LOVER

One month later, at Sonder:

Maliyan stared at Luna to see if there was any sign of him returning to his longtime love, Mr Marijuana.

"I'm still off it," said Luna with annoyance.

"Great," said Maliyan.

"Did you think I'd get back on it?" asked Luna.

Maliyan didn't want to say yes, but Luna had been quite changeable in the past.

"He's a hard lover to dump," shrugged Maliyan.

"I haven't gone through all this for nothing," said Luna emphatically.

Maliyan smiled approvingly at the unsmoked, defogged, cleaner, clearer version of Luna sitting beside her.

Two tradies waited outside Sonder for their takeaway. They leaned on the wall casually, their strong, bare legs seeming not to notice the bitter wind. Luna's seven months in the city had noticeably brought out his gayness. He was living and working in an area where he was not only free to express it, but encouraged to. He eyed off the ruggedly handsome men. He did it so openly and unashamedly that even though both men were probably straight, they took it as a compliment and laughed.

Maliyan, on the other hand, looked away. It wasn't that she was jealous or embarrassed. She didn't want to give any energy to Luna's highly flirtatious ways. He flirted with everyone—no one was left out. He wasn't a serious flirt. If anyone pursued the offer for more than ten seconds, he exited the scene. He had many chances to follow through with interested parties on both sides of the track and rarely took them up. This quality of non-neediness made his flirtations funny and endearing rather than unwanted.

Nevertheless, as Luna was becoming an unfogged being, Maliyan wanted him to keep going in that direction. If she laughed at his flirtations, it would have fueled the behaviour. If she looked even a minuscule jealous, it surely would have ignited it. The best approach seemed not to have an opinion about it. In that way, she was neither feeding nor resisting it, liking nor disliking it. We don't have to have an opinion about everything. And sometimes, the most helpful thing is not to.

CHAPTER 11

PRINCESS

"How's everything at your house? asked Luna.

"Bell-Bell's coming from Nanima in a few days," said Maliyan.

"That's nice," said Luna.

"Not really," said Maliyan.

Last spring, Bell-Bell decided not to sell her father's house and asked Maliyan to keep looking after it in exchange for cheap rent. She also wanted to visit Black Forest every few months. The visits were becoming less enjoyable for Maliyan, who had thought about alternative rentals, but nothing affordable was available.

"She's a princess," said Maliyan flatly.

"Well, yeah, that's obvious," said Luna. "What does her partner do about it?"

"Nothing," said Maliyan. "I guess he wanted a princess."

"If they are both happy..." said Luna.

"Who is happy with that?" said Maliyan. "If you are the master, you alternate between being satisfied with your servant and resenting that they are weak. If you are the servant, you alternate between being glad of having a god and resenting your lack of dignity. Not to mention, sex needs equals."

"You *did* mention it," said Luna.

"She can do better," said Maliyan.

"Better partner?" asked Luna.

"Partner is not the point," said Maliyan.

"Have you talked about it with her?" asked Luna.

"It goes very badly," said Maliyan. "Instead of being a straightforward princess, she turns into a psychological princess throwing justifications and veiled insults around left, right, and centre with her intelligent, offended brain."

"Then, don't do it," said Luna.

"That would be the end of the friendship," said Maliyan. "Anyway, I made a commitment to help her and I can't abandon that unless she makes it perfectly clear that she wishes it to be so."

"If you can't talk to her," said Luna, "it's not much of a friendship."

"Exactly," said Maliyan.

CHAPTER 12

TO A TEA

Early morning, a few days later:

"Got your chai on the way, lovely Maliyan," said Tim.

He and his brother, Tom, ran their Black Forest cafe, *To a Tea,* from their shop window. They had their operating system down to a tee. Tim was a bubbly, affable fellow who was great with all the different types of townsfolk who came his way. At forty, with a family of young kids, he was old enough to know the struggles of life but young enough to tolerate people's stupidity without complaint. He complained to his brother without restraint, but that was behind closed doors.

Tom stayed at the coffee machine. He didn't cope well with people, although, at home, he was happy enough. He kept his head down and focused on the more manageable coffee. There were some exceptions, and he walked the few steps from the coffee machine to the cafe window to deliver the coffee personally. Maliyan realised that he made this decision the first few times a new person came to the shop, and it rarely changed. On her second visit, he walked to the window and personally handed her order to her. Naturally, she would have taken no notice, but she saw that Tim stopped working and smiled knowingly. After that, both men called her *lovely Maliyan* whenever she went to the shop.

CHAPTER 13

DEAD WRONG

"I didn't get you a coffee," Maliyan said to Bell after returning home from To a Tea. "I thought you would still be doing your meditation practice."

"I'm better without it," said Bell, who had a highly reactive body.

Bell-Bell was reactive to many things, physical and mental. She said it was because of her neurodivergency. Maliyan tried to tell her that some issues had little to do with neurodiversity and much to do with the neurotypical functioning of the ego. However, it always resulted in some type of meltdown from Bell. Thus, the cycle continued, getting nowhere.

When it came to the few people Maliyan let into her inner circle, they could be any manner of thing on the outside, but inside, they had to have two clear orientations towards her. Firstly, they had to have a sincere, heartfelt love for her. It didn't have to be a perfect love by any stretch of the imagination, but it had to be the sort of love that if she weren't there anymore, they would suffer the loss deeply.

Secondly, they had to have an instinctive respect for her knowingness about certain aspects of life. There were countless things Maliyan didn't know, and in many areas, she was quite ignorant. But the essence of life, the nature of people, the evolution of individual consciousness—this she knew. If they couldn't see that or chose not to, competed with it, or belittled it, then she could not waste herself on them. They didn't have to understand anything about what Maliyan knew, but they had to trust it enough not to dismiss her efforts to help them. Maliyan didn't doubt that Bell fulfilled the first condition, but the second was dismantling before her eyes.

That evening, before retiring to bed, Bell said, "I know that you are trying to help, but the thing is, I know better than you about me."

It sounded so reasonable and said with the considered, educated tact of a psychologically sophisticated person. But both knew, it was dead wrong.

CHAPTER 14

AS FAR AS PARTNERS GO

he next day:

"How's Luna?" asked Bell as Maliyan drove her to the airport for her return flight to Nanima.

"He's doing well," said Maliyan cautiously.

"Do you see him much?" asked Bell, trying to sound casual.

This was a no-win conversation. Nothing about it could help their flailing relationship. Although it was never spoken of, Maliyan had long sensed that Bell was interested in a couple relationship with her. Bell was like that. She had loose boundaries when it came to conventional living, which is one of the things Maliyan valued about her. However, Maliyan did not want that sort of relationship with her. Also, Bell had a perfectly good partner, as far as partners go. Regardless, changing partners wouldn't have helped.

If Maliyan had killed the idea earlier, there was a high chance that Bell would have aborted the whole relationship. Maliyan didn't want her to do that. Just because someone misunderstands how their path will unfold does not mean that they cannot, with time, accept and understand it. It takes perseverance and humility on the part of the path-taker and wisdom and timing on the part of the path-guide.

Bell was barking up the wrong tree for her evolution and happiness. There was something more valuable for her to gain than she could currently imagine. However, she first needed to transcend the fear and anger of her mental meltdowns. She needed to let down her years of carefully crafted defence. Would she be able to do that? Probably not. Not on her own. But last spring, she took a thread from Geboor—her thread. It was the thread that Francis spoke about in his Nanima poustinia.

> Everything is stored in
> the fabric of Geboor.
> Take a thread and
> pull it towards you.
> Not any thread.
> If you take the wrong one,
> it will fray away.
>
> Take the thread that is yours.
> Tie it around you.
> See how it remains anchored
> in the bowels of Geboor.
> Wind it around you so
> many times, you forget that
> once it was not a part of you.

At the time, Bell said, "The thread is much less *me* than I imagined it would be."

The *lessening* of Bell had begun and was now intensifying.

CHAPTER 15

WHEN EVERYONE IS GOOD

The twin-engine propellor plane taking Bell back home from Black Forest had ten passengers. With ten rows of three seats, everyone had a row to themselves. That was exactly as Bell and the other country passengers had anticipated. It was a little bumpy, as small planes tend to be, but stress-free and hugely quicker than an all-day drive.

The good-looking flight attendant served tea and snacks and asked each person how their day was going. His easy country smile was placid and generous. Whenever anyone asked him in return how his day was, he said happily, "I'm good when everyone else is good." He looked pleased with his philosophy, glad that as a rural lad of probably twenty-eight, he had come up with such a magnanimous approach to life. It genuinely did seem as if nothing much from inside him would ruffle him. Yet, somehow, his approach bothered Bell, who took it upon herself to educate him.

"That is a nice approach," said Bell, "but, you know, everyone has a right to their own feelings."

The host listened politely, thought for a moment, and said, "Would you like more tea or another biscuit?"

Bell decided to leave him alone.

The plane flew at a height of around 10,000 feet, well below the path of commercial jets. The winter countryside below was quite visible at that height and gave a delightful passing show of green hills and small towns. However, it didn't create much delight in Bell, although she felt it should.

CHAPTER 16

RING THE BELL

As the plane approached Thubbo airport, Bell's eyes traced the Wambul's watery course snaking through dreamland country. Once onboard the XPT to Nanima (the express passenger train), Bell again crossed paths with the river as it forged its way under railway bridges of clickity-clack metal and wood. The Wambul was moving in the opposite direction to her, having come from Nanima, where it had collected the Bell River.

The introduction of the rural XPT a few decades ago significantly improved travel time and comfort from Thubbo to the city, Nanima being its second stop. There was a choice of tickets—regular and first class. It seemed to Bell that there was no viable difference between a first-class and regular ticket. Nevertheless, she always spent a few extra dollars to get the first-class one. She had learned that, as one passenger put it, "First class gets rid of the riff-raff." Bell thought it was strange that for a few dollars, you could decide if you were worthy of the peace and quiet of a first-class ride or rough it a bit with the regular folk. First class was rarely full.

The train driver beeped at a lone roadworker on a nearby dirt track. The worker looked up and waved. Later, the driver blew his whistle at a farmer working his field on a tractor. Further on, he acknowledged a tradie on the roof of a dairy close to the railway track. The driver didn't whistle at groups of workers, only lone ones. Bell thought it was a way of saying, *Hey buddy, you are not alone. I see you.*

A woman sitting beside her started a conversation and commented that Bell-Bell was an unusual name.

"My real name is Laura-Bella," explained Bell, "but I was given the name Bell-Bell and tend to use it."

"You are in the right place with a name like that," said the woman.

"I guess so," said Bell.

Ignoring Bell's lack of enthusiasm, the woman continued, "I'm on my way to Nanima for Landcare Week. We are focusing on the Bell River erosion problems and launching a program called *Ring the Bell,* which will educate the farmers and townsfolk on how to best preserve the river."

"Perhaps it will help raise funds for the restoration of the low-lying bridge that got washed away in the flood two years ago," said Bell.

"Yes," said the woman, "but more important than the bridge is the river itself. We are destroying it. The collapse of the bridge is just a symptom. The junction of the Bell and Wambul Rivers is in crisis due to manmade erosion. People have pulled out the vegetation from the riverbanks, which has sped up the water. That, in turn, has meant the relentless cutting away of the rivers' banks and cliffs, and acres of topsoil have been washed away."

Listening to the woman's devoted and unselfish care for the land helped Bell to somewhat forget about her own problems.

"One of our educators did a little demonstration by putting an empty saucepan on a burning BBQ, and it quickly became hot," said the woman. "He then added water to the pot and explained how it slowed down the heating process. Lastly, he added some soil to slow the process down further. The moral of the story is that we need soil, trees, and healthy waterways, or not only will our manmade constructs be washed away, but we ourselves will ultimately perish."

THREE STRIKES

CHAPTER 17

DATE DAY

A *few days later, in Black Forest:*

It was a thrilling, sunny day—cold but glorious. A blue winter's day in Black Forest shines with brilliance against the backdrop of gloom. A week after Luna's last visit, he decided to drive out to Black Forest again and soak in the clear, smog-free sunshine. After their Sonder catch-up, they went for a creek walk. Iggy romped through the long, wet grass with the enthusiasm of a farm dog just let off his chain. Luna and Maliyan had nothing but happiness to share with each other. The spirited creek inspired more than usual depth in their conversation. All in all, a brilliant day.

TEXT MESSAGE FROM LUNA THAT EVENING

Hi boo. Had such a great day, I've decided I'll come out weekly from now on. It will be good for me.

MALIYAN

Great! I'd love that.

LUNA

It's a date then!

CHAPTER 18

CATCHING

The next week approached, and there was no message from Luna.

MALIYAN

Are we catching up?

No reply. If Luna didn't want to talk, he simply didn't answer. A lot of men do that.

NOT READY TO CONCEDE DEFEAT, MALIYAN TRIED AGAIN the following day.

MALIYAN

Hi, love. Come out if you can. Iggy wants to be a country dog!

Nothing.

CHAPTER 19

FUEL FOR GROWTH

Although Luna was loved by many people for his widespread exuberance towards them, it wasn't by accident that he was still single. He was marvellous at intermittent relationships, not consistent ones. He said it was his parent's fault for modelling bad relationship behaviour. Maliyan didn't correct him because she was still in the stage of encouraging him to speak about things that he normally didn't speak about. However, one day, she would tell him, "If you grew up in a less-than-fortunate situation, then it needs to be turned into fuel for growth, not uncorrected bad behaviour."

Luna's inconsistency stemmed from his changeableness. Fluidity of thought can be a sign of an expansive mind, which is good. However, it can also be a sign of a fractured mind, which is not. If we want to get somewhere in life, we have to walk in a straight line (or, at least, a curving, back-and-forth one). We can't walk in circles, or we will never get anywhere. Luna tended to walk in circles. Maliyan trusted the core of Luna's heart, but outwardly, he could be irrationally and often insultingly contradictory.

The way he introduced her was a point in question. One day, when he was in a belittling frame of mind, he and Maliyan ran into someone outside Sonder. Luna introduced Maliyan as his "customer from Luna Tiks"! Sometimes, he introduced her as one of his besties. It could vary wildly. Maliyan suspected that the most complimentary he was of her was to other people, out of her earshot, to those she didn't know and would never know. Somehow, it would have seemed safer to Luna. Of course, it was a protective mechanism, but that did not lessen the destructiveness of the behaviour.

Earlier in the year, Maliyan had suggested that for the next get-together, they go to a nearby town, somewhere other than Sonder. Luna agreed. The day of the outing arrived. Maliyan was excited about the new adventure and messaged Luna before he left the city.

MALIYAN

Don't forget a coat in case the weather turns.

He didn't reply, but she assumed he was already on his way. When he arrived, he immediately headed into Sonder to order for them both. Realising that they were not going anywhere, and he hadn't even told her, Maliyan felt embarrassed and humiliated. Humiliation is a great silencer. It would have seemed pathetic to object, like a child waiting for a party invitation that never arrives. Isn't that how people are played, consciously or unconsciously? Take away the capacity for humiliation, and there is nothing left to play with. It may have been fear on Luna's part, but it was harmful and hurtful.

CHAPTER 20

BUSY BOO

T*he following week:*

MALIYAN

I haven't heard from you in 2 weeks. Is everything fine? Are you coming out to Black Forest?

LUNA (THE NEXT DAY)

Sorry boo. Been busy. Will let you know. I think so. But will have to see.

THREE STRIKES, HE'S OUT!

PART III
BECOMING
SPRING

CLOSED EYES

CHAPTER 21

WHERE RIVERS MEET

In Nanima:

Luna's old cafe, Luna Tiks, had been bought and renovated by a local entrepreneurial family. The husband owned a real estate business, and the wife owned the cafe, now called *Where Rivers Meet*. It had a completely different feel to Luna Tiks—spacious, tastefully decorated with home decor items, and with a fire to add charm and warmth. The old shophouse that Luna had lived in was now part of the refurbished cafe. *Where Rivers Meet* was a hit with visitors and townsfolk. Even those who missed Luna had been mostly won over.

As Bell watched the steady spring rain through the cafe's clean window, a waitress approached and said, "Isn't it beautiful? I love it when it rains like this."

Bell mused that in Black Forest, the general response to yet another day of rain and greyness was commiseration. Here in Nanima, the rain was needed and appreciated, especially steady rain—consistent enough to soak deep into the earth but not manic enough to cause floods and wash away a year's income.

The waitress was a healthy, robust, twenty-year-old girl with no makeup and a fresh, straightforward face that looked like it would never be happier than jumping out of a Land Rover to open gates and rescue stray sheep. Something about the girl's uncomplicated happiness gave Bell an idea.

CHAPTER 22

RAIN ON ME

After walking to the junction of the Bell and Wambul, Bell followed the track upstream until she got to Euroka's hut.

"To what do I owe the pleasure of your company?" asked Euroka.

As his face was expressionless, Bell couldn't tell if he was making fun of her or complimenting her.

"Good to see you again," said Bell. "I was wondering if you had some spare time for me. I'm doing well, but…"

"If you are doing well, why do you need me?" asked Euroka.

Bell stiffened and said, "Will you help?"

Euroka turned his gaze to his beloved river and watched the rain make patterns on its skin.

"Come tomorrow morning at 6:00 a.m. for two hours," said Euroka, "and every morning after that for a week."

He didn't wait for a response but returned to his hut and left Bell alone in the rain.

CHAPTER 23

NO RESPONSE

When Bell arrived at Euroka's the following morning, he indicated for her to sit cross-legged under a gum tree next to the river.

"Two hours," he commanded. "Don't get up. Don't close your eyes. If I see them closed, that's the end."

"Don't close my eyes?" protested Bell.

"Last warning—don't speak either," said Euroka, closing his hut door.

Luckily, Bell had a naturally flexible body and could sit cross-legged without undue stress. Not closing her eyes was more problematic. She had to admit that she did have a tendency to fall asleep or daydream when her eyes were closed.

The first hour was spent ranting in her head about Euroka:

- Isn't he grateful that I came to him?
- Doesn't he realise that I am an advanced spiritual student?
- Why does he have to be so condescending?
- Maybe it was a mistake to come here.
- It was definitely a mistake.
- It's not like he is inundated with people asking for his help.
- I'll show him!

After an hour, Euroka appeared. Bell had momentarily closed her eyes (maybe more than a moment), but his noise jolted them open. He potted around his vegetable patch, appearing to take no notice of her, and then went back inside. It started raining.

Another hour to go, thought Bell. *And I'm getting wet. And I feel worse than before I started. I think I'll leave and not even tell him.*

A kookaburra laughed in a branch high above her. It stopped Bell's train of thought. She looked at the river, which seemed elated with the wet weather. Recalling the thread she pulled from Geboor, a subtle sense of acceptance entered her body. It was like a distant ship, so far away that one questions its existence. Bell tried to pull it closer, but it disappeared over the horizon, and she returned to her former mental state. Not exactly the same. She was a touch more settled. Partially accepting that she was going to be wet, uncomfortable, and couldn't close her eyes, the next hour passed slowly but surely. When the time was up, she stood, stretched, and knocked on Euroka's door. No response.

OPEN EYES

Every morning at 6:00 am, Bell returned to the river, although all but the last morning were touch and go as to whether she would turn up or not. On the final day, although nothing had changed and Euroka was as unengaged as at the beginning, she felt calm as she sat cross-legged, open-eyed, watching the river, and being quite prepared that she would end up wet again. The rain was in no hurry to leave.

"If you wish, you may close your eyes today," said Euroka.

Although Bell had been dying to close her eyes all week (maybe as an escape, maybe in the hope of finding relief or being blessed), now that she was allowed to, she was not especially driven to do so. When she did close them, she found it wasn't particularly different from having them open. Or was it the other way around—that eyes open wasn't different to eyes closed? Either way, she knew it was progress.

"You may feel that I'm harsh on you," said Euroka at

the end of the session. "Take it as a compliment. I do not waste my time and energy."

Bell couldn't help but glow inside. One such comment from Euroka was worth fourteen hours of sitting in the rain rudderless.

"When you think you're going well," said Euroka, "you're generally going poorly. And when you feel deflated, you're often much closer to making progress. You have created such a thick defence that it has become your greatest enemy. It is all one big, stupid, unnecessary lump of fear. Don't you see how the river watches over you? Don't you hear how the kookaburra keeps you amused? Once you learn that your fear is entirely unnecessary, your potential will blossom."

Ever since Euroka returned from Uluru two years ago, certain things about him had changed inexplicably. For one thing, his style of speech was more eloquent and sophisticated, as if he had undergone a whole system of education while away (although that was not possible because he had only been gone for a few months).

Maybe he downloaded it at Uluru, Bell thought.

She was about to say she could already feel her potential blossoming, but Euroka continued. "When you sit with the river long enough—not sleeping, not making things up, just sitting, just being—there is a chance of becoming, a chance of becoming something more until, one day, you become the river."

HOME AWAY FROM HOME

CHAPTER 25

DREAM HOME

Maliyan couldn't remember if the strangely familiar place first became known to her in a dream or a meditation. It didn't matter because some dreams are meditative, and some meditations are dreamy. The place was becoming more familiar with repeat appearances. It was home, a different home to Earth, a place of belonging. As far as Maliyan knew, it didn't have a name. It was not necessary. Things were known by a nameless sort of energy. The places and people there were recognised by their unique energy combinations.

The dream-meditation always began in the same way, with a distant song that was profoundly known, yet Maliyan could never quite put her finger on the tune or the lyrics. It was singing of something she knew to be precious, but if she concentrated, it would fade and become inaudible.

The planet was similar to Earth but with more variety of lifeforms and greater intensity. Intensity of what? Colour, energy, ability to create. In their physical form, most people loosely resembled humans, which suited the planet in the same way humans suit Earth. However, unlike humans, a lot of time was spent in their invisible energy bodies. There was a great variety of physical forms, which added to the fun of the place.

CHAPTER 26

FAMILY

And there was family. Maliyan's "parents" were parents to many. They were very tall, whitish, and extremely benevolent. She felt highly protected and nurtured in their presence, as did everyone. Most people lived alone, although no one ever felt lonely because the entire population was highly connected. If they wanted to talk to someone, all they had to do was think of them, and the conversation began. It began even if the other person was otherwise occupied because they could all manage numerous realities simultaneously.

The planet's inhabitants lived in homes made from natural substances readily available in the environment, such as wood, grass, and mud. The houses merged into the landscape unobtrusively and seemed to disappear when not needed. No one lived in big houses with empty rooms. Everyone's house was exactly the size they needed, so not too much time was spent looking after them.

Each person also cared for their surrounding land, usually a few acres. Food was cultivated on the acreage. It was perfectly aligned with the resident's needs. The longer they lived there, the more in sync the food became. They also had herb patches for medicines when needed. Anything else required was ordered from small local depots, which were every ten kilometres. There were no cities or towns. There were no cars as the residents all walked or sometimes teleported. There was no pollution. There was also no type of predatory nature, even amongst the animals. Nature was in perfect balance.

The population of the planet was significantly less than Earth's at about one billion. It was kept steady at that size, although no one was forbidden to reproduce. Residents could volunteer for the assignment. Generally, those with the desire to reproduce had excellent DNA and outstanding nurturing qualities. In the bulk of people, the desire for sex and reproduction was largely dormant, although it could be activated if one chose. Usually, it was left unactivated so that energy was channelled into other areas of life. No more than one offspring came from one family grouping. Parenting was a mutual and karmic decision to dedicate twenty years of their existence to child-raising. Regardless, the two tall beings were still known to everyone as ultimate parents, and their DNA was in all beings on the planet. So, in that sense, they truly were everyone's parents.

CHAPTER 27

TENANTS

One of the planet's primary functions was to help less developed planets in other galaxies. Earth was definitely considered underdeveloped and in dire need of assistance. Half the population of the dream planet (half being 500 million) spent a substantial part of their lifespan (a lifespan was generally 200 years) dedicating themselves to the growth of other planets. As so many residents had "jobs" requiring them to travel to other galaxies, the planet seemed to have a much lower population than it actually had. When Maliyan was there, she was aware that Earth was an impossibly long way away by human standards, but the inhabitants of the dream planet had far superior forms of transport to Earth and found the distance no problem or barrier.

Everyone on the planet had long ago learned to live peacefully, intelligently, and lovingly. Although there were different opinions, no one ever fought. Ever. Also, the concept of ownership didn't exist. Everyone was a tenant —of property and even more so of relationships. This entirely removed the demands, frictions, jealousies, disappointments, tyrannies, and endless problems that Earth people usually experience. It meant that the dream planet inhabitants had an innate honesty in their communications. There was nothing to hide because each person's path was respected and trusted, including one's own.

WHEN MALIYAN WOKE ONE MORNING AFTER VISITING her dream home, she recalled an Earth interview with movie star Nicole Kidman shortly after separating from her famous husband, Tom Cruise. Kidman said that although they had houses all over the world, not one of them felt like home. The comment always stayed in Maliyan's mind as a reminder that a home has nothing to do with a house. Houses cost money. Homes cost your spirit. Some homes, such as Maliyan's dream home, cost the recollection of your boundless and multidimensional nature.

TYE AND BYE

CHAPTER 28

BYE

In Black Forest:

Ronny, the co-owner of Sonder, looked at Maliyan oddly from his post behind the coffee machine. When it was her turn to order, he left his post and told the waitress that he'd do this one.

"I'm not sick," said Maliyan, pointing to her face mask.

Ronny shrugged to reassure her that it was fine.

"I've been to Dr Tye in The Flat," said Maliyan.

"Respected by many people," said Ronny, "including me."

"I had to have a spot removed from my face, so I'm covering it with this mask," explained Maliyan.

"You still look beautiful," said Ronny in a totally uncharacteristic way for his standoffish manner.

He then walked back to the coffee machine and let the girl take everyone else's orders.

It was not until the following week that Maliyan could make sense of Ronny's curious behaviour. Sonder had new owners. It was his goodbye.

CHAPTER 29

DR TYE

In The Flat:

The Flat was the next town citybound to Black Forest. It was presumably named after the river flats on which the town was built. Unlike the dense tree population of Black Forest, The Flat was a rolling green valley. In Black Forest, the trees lived so close to you that you could hear them breathing. In The Flat, you could see the ever-changing expanse of sky.

When Maliyan returned to The Flat to get her stitches out, Dr Tye was his normal attentive self.

"How are you?" he asked, entering the room.

THE FIRST THING MALIYAN HAD NOTICED ABOUT DR Tye was the way he said, *"How are you?"* Many people ask the question without even looking at you, let alone waiting for an answer. Dr Tye not only looked at you but waited for a response and then listened to what you said. It was such an unusual trait that when he first did it, Maliyan didn't respond. She was used to thinking, *Why waste your breath responding to questions that people have no interest in knowing the answer to?* After an awkward silence, she realised that Dr Tye was waiting. "Oh, ahh, good," she spluttered. "Yes, good. Thanks!"

❧

BACK TO TODAY:

"I'm going well," replied Maliyan. "Thanks for asking. And you?"

"Let's get those stitches out," said Dr Tye as he reached for his scissors.

Although he attentively listened to other people's problems, he didn't burden his patients with his own.

CHAPTER 30

ROLE REVERSAL

In To a Tea:

Maliyan's morning cafe stops alternated between Sonder and To a Tea. She wanted to support both and enjoyed the different ambiance of each. Sonder, being a transplant of a city cafe, had upmarket, trendy attention to detail. However, the true-blue, country-bloke nature of the two To a Tea brothers (who knew everything and everyone of local interest) had a simple charm that held equal value.

Recently, the To a Tea brothers had made a small indoor seating area. As they were trying to coax customers out of their window ordering habit, Maliyan had taken to sitting indoors. Sometimes, she was the only one sitting there. As she was making no noise, the brothers would forget she was there and start speaking amongst themselves in their brotherly banter—more swearing, more complaining, and a surprising role reversal. At the window, Tim (the younger brother) was the frontman, the protector, the voice. In private, Tom upheld his older brother status as steadier, reassurer, confidant, and guide.

"Bye, boys," said Maliyan on her way out.

"Oh, bye, lovely Maliyan," said Tim. "Apologies for the language. We forgot you were there."

CHAPTER 31

STAYING ALIVE

In Sonder:

Someone who definitely preferred the upmarket trendiness of Sonder was a woman Maliyan later came to know as Leteisha—well-mannered, quick to compliment, dressed with tasteful money, educated, and entirely pleasant. The reason she caught Maliyan's eye was because an interesting story was unfolding.

Maliyan initially noticed the effort Leteisha put into thanking the cafe staff and smiling at people she knew and even those she didn't (including Maliyan). However, there was an underlying nervousness, bordering on anxiety, that lay below the surface. Maliyan also noticed that Leteisha had a wedding ring, but she had never seen a husband with her. Leteisha was the sort of person who could easily attract a great partner and also the sort of person to need one.

Then, a man started sitting with her. He was about her age (fiftyish), confident, relaxed, and at ease with the world. As the weeks and months passed, it went from an occasional catch-up to a daily occurrence. The man certainly wasn't Leteisha's husband. They were too wide-eyed engaged. There was too much excitement between them. They were also careful, like when you walk at breaking dawn and can't clearly see the ground ahead. Not a husband. Nor a friend—friends aren't *that* exciting.

Leteisha was obviously falling in love with the man (obvious to Maliyan, perhaps not to all the other table occupants in Sonder). At first, it was tentative and guarded. Then, throwing the good sense of fifty years into the wind, it was an exuberant fall into falling in love. Fortunately, the man also seemed to share the feeling, even if a little less...

What is it less of? wondered Maliyan. *Desperate. Desperate? That's weird. Leteisha is not a desperate woman. So, why does something feel desperate?*

Soon after, Maliyan was told by a local that Leteisha's only son, a young man of twenty, had been killed in a car accident. She also found out that Leteisha's husband was Dr Tye! Beautiful Dr Tye.

Oh no, thought Maliyan. *Poor Dr Tye. He lost his son and now his wife. And maybe he doesn't even know he has lost his wife.*

Maliyan did not blame Leteisha. She and Dr Tye would have had a marriage as wonderful and successful as they both were. But when a child dies, a mother has to find a reason to...stay alive.

I COULD SEE PEACE

CHAPTER 32

NEITHER GOOD NOR BAD

TEXT FROM LUNA

Hi angel. I'm coming out to see Dr Tye in The Flat tomorrow. If you are around and feel like a catch-up, I'll drive to Black Forest after the appointment.

MALIYAN

Sure. See you tomorrow.

n Black Forest:

It had been several months since their last Sonder rendezvous. When Maliyan saw Luna, any thought of him playing her went out the window. From the expression on his face and the feel of his energy, the only person he had been playing was himself. And he wasn't enjoying it.

"If you could see me the way I see myself," sighed Luna, "you wouldn't like me. I suppose you only see yourself as a good person."

"I don't see myself as a person at all," said Maliyan.

"I didn't have the heart to tell you," said Luna, "but I got back on the weed."

"And Dr Tye?" asked Maliyan.

"He's helping me with some sleeping pills while I get off it again," said Luna. "The doctor I went to in the city was a d***head and said I'd get addicted to the sleeping pills just like I was to the marijuana. I felt worse than when I walked into his office, and that was pretty damn bad. It's all just so f***ing hard."

He put his head in his hands.

After an extended silence, Maliyan said, "Let's go for a walk."

They quietly talked about things of no particular consequence as they followed the creek's winding course. And with each watery bend, the struggle dissipated into the clean air of the breathing trees.

CHAPTER 33

ALL CONCERNED

"Hello, darling," said Bell as Maliyan answered the phone. "How are you?"

"Great to hear from you," said Maliyan. "I was wondering how things were going for you back in Nanima."

It was a few months since Bell's last visit to Black Forest.

"I know I can be honest with you," said Bell.

That's a good start, thought Maliyan.

"When I got back home, I felt terrible," said Bell. "Then, in the first week of spring, still feeling terrible, I went down to Euroka, and he gave me a retreat program. Really, it was just sitting by the Bell. I'm not so ignorant as to not realise that sitting in the presence of someone like Euroka (particularly since his Uluru journey) can impact a person greatly."

"And did it?" asked Maliyan.

"At first, I thought it didn't help me much, which was disappointing. But then I noticed that the tide had turned. More than just turning around, certain things in my mind became clear to me in a way I had never been able to grasp before."

"What were they?" asked Maliyan with genuine excitement.

"It was more of a losing something than gaining something," said Bell. "It was a lessening rather than an increasing, but, oh, how much better I feel."

"That's wonderful," said Maliyan.

"The day after my retreat," said Bell, "I was walking along the Bell River to the shops, and a thought came to me. It has stayed with me ever since."

"What was it?" asked Maliyan.

"I could see peace instead of what I see right now," said Bell. "It seems simple, doesn't it? Such a little thing. Swap the complaint, anger, and fear thought for a peaceful one that isn't complaining, isn't angry, and isn't afraid. Simple, but, by God, not easy. It was only because I felt so bad that I gave it a real shot."

"That's beautiful," said Maliyan.

"The whole thing made me feel significantly more settled. I didn't have to be right or wrong about anything. It was irrelevant. I didn't have to work out what to do. And I stopped thinking about my relationship. I don't mean that in a bad way, but I stopped endlessly ruminating about it. What a relief. *Everything* has been going so much better, and I've had many creative ideas. I must have made some space for them."

After a long pause, Bell said, "Enough of me! How are you?"

"Going well, love," said Maliyan. "The weather has greatly improved. Spring has been divine. When are you visiting next?"

"That brings me to my next point," said Bell. "You

know how I was going to sell my father's house last spring but changed my mind after visiting Geboor and pulling my thread from the mountain?"

"Yes," said Maliyan.

"Now that my mind is clearer and I am calmer," said Bell, "I have decided to sell my father's house after all, which means, of course, that you will have to move. I'd like it sold by summer, if possible."

"Not long then," said Maliyan.

"I shouldn't say I *decided* to sell my father's house," said Bell. "It was one of the ideas that became obvious of its own accord."

"In that case," said Maliyan, "it will be the right idea— for you, for me, and for all concerned."

PART IV
THE FLAT
SUMMER AGAIN

GUIDING LIGHT

FROM ABOVE

It was 4 a.m. and Maliyan was driving from Black Forest to The Flat. The car was so full that she couldn't see out the back window, but it didn't matter because no one else was on the road. The sky was clear, and the stars were in all their glory. Luna sometimes said that the middle-of-the-night stars were the best because you didn't have to share them with anyone else. Maliyan thought that the stars were like love. They don't diminish with shining.

Bell sold her father's house, and in perfect synchronicity, the right one appeared in The Flat for Maliyan. It had a paddock at the back of the house that reached the creek below. The house was at one of the town's entrances, but being a country town, the shops were still very walkable.

As Maliyan had woken at 3:30 a.m. (wide awake), she thought it best to get up and start transporting her belongings because it was moving day. When she pulled up at her new rental, the stars seemed to glow even more brightly. They were such good company and so reassuring. How could one ever feel alone with that much tender light from above guiding the way?

CHAPTER 35

FOOLPROOF

There is a guiding principle in life that tells us to follow our loves. What are our loves? Anything that creates a passion, a fire, an instinctive interest in us. Follow it. When you have choices before you, follow the one that creates the most amount of enthusiasm in you. If it is a tiny fire, still follow it. Passion is your creator's way of letting you know which way to go. It is foolproof. Follow it wholeheartedly and use everything you have to make it work.

However, there is another guiding principle of equal importance. If you reach a brick wall, don't bang your head on it. You will only hurt yourself. The longer you keep banging, the more blood there will be. It is there for a reason. The road ahead wasn't going to work. Wipe the blood away, dust yourself down, dry your tears, and take a moment to assimilate your loss. Then, turn in a different direction and keep moving. Up ahead, unbeknown to you, is a clear road waiting for your footsteps.

Use both of these guiding principles—follow your passion but don't insist on the outcome—and your path will lead around all the obstacles and bring you to majestic vistas.

MALIYAN

Alright.

LUNA

Please don't think it's you. It's not. It's me.

MALIYAN

There's no question of who it is.

SILENCE.

MALIYAN

The thing is, Luna, you make me nervous. You do and say so many thinly-covered, dismissive and insulting things that I have to prepare myself to get hurt. I know that's not the kind of relationship you want with me, but that's what's happening. So, it's better you go than do things you regret. Safe travels, and I love you, too.

SYNCHRONISTIC SIGNS

CHAPTER 36

HAPPY BIRTHDAY

n The Flat:

As Maliyan entered the cake shop, Dr Tye held the door open and said, "Hi, Maliyan, nice to see you."

"Someone's birthday?" asked Maliyan, pointing to the cake with *Happy Birthday* written on the top.

"Yes," said Dr Tye.

He was about to leave but stepped back inside and moved away from the door traffic. His eyes were downcast.

"It's my son's birthday," he said. "He died a few years ago."

He then looked at Maliyan piercingly with the unlikely hope she may have some magic way of lessening the pain. Maliyan met his gaze, which was as pain-drenched as any gaze could be. She didn't move, didn't flinch, didn't say anything. Some things cannot be carried by words, but to know that another human is not afraid to see our pain—as it is, in its raw, ridiculous horror—somehow makes it more bearable.

"I still don't have words..." said Dr Tye.

Maliyan nodded.

The moment of torture softened its grip, and Dr Tye went to the counter and asked for a knife. He cut a large piece of cake and handed it to Maliyan in a serviette.

"Are you sure?" asked Maliyan politely.

Dr Tye nodded and said, "There's only me to eat it."

CHAPTER 37

DROP THE DOCTOR

Over the next few days, Maliyan ran into Dr Tye three times: once at the cafe, once at the super-market, and once at the bank.

"Three times lucky," said Dr Tye as he pulled his cash from the automatic teller.

"Hello again, Dr Tye," said Maliyan.

"Please, drop the doctor. It's Tye."

Maliyan smiled.

After a quick chat, he said, "I'm going to the new Thai restaurant tonight. Would you like to try it, too?"

"I don't really eat at night..." said Maliyan. "But, sure, why not?"

At the end of a delicious and relaxed dinner, Tye walked Maliyan to her car and said, "Thank you. I enjoyed that. Maybe we could do it again?"

Maliyan thought for a moment and said, "Could I please say something?"

"Of course," said Tye maturely.

"If you want a friend, I could be that. If you want a close friend, I could probably be that too, but I'm not girl-friend or partner material."

Tye was an intelligent and considerate man, but he was also a fairly conventional one, at least compared to Maliyan. She knew she was pushing the boundaries of what he could cope with by having this conversation, but she felt it was worse to put him in a position where he could be hurt. Besides, if he actually did want to be friends, he had to show that he was willing to meet some amount of mental challenge without immediately bailing.

"You could easily find a lovely woman," continued Maliyan. "Good company, someone to care about you, share stories with and talk to about your day. Maybe even someone to share more than that if it worked out that way. I'm not that person. I'm more monk than anything else. I only look normal on the outside."

Tye made a face as if to say, *Do you look normal?* Both laughed, breaking the awkwardness of the conversation. See what a good man he was? He knew how to make the conversation easier and cared enough to do so. Neverthe-less, he got the point, and Maliyan felt relieved.

Although Maliyan understood Tye's desire to re-part-ner, which would be exacerbated by seeing his wife in love with someone else, she felt he was capable of more. Would re-partnering fix his problems? Would it take away his pain? Would it guarantee him personal happiness? At the beginning, maybe. But for how long?

There is nothing intrinsically wrong with seeking a couple relationship. It fulfils many needs, but the concept of a romantic relationship as the highest pinnacle of life, worthy of all the hype, is faulty. And once in it, most people become so focused on its maintenance that it monopolises their attention for the rest of their life. If Tye resisted the urge to run after it and turned inwards to investigate the essence of his own life, then his rewards would be disproportionally great. Later, after he found his way in new territory, if he wanted someone, then he wouldn't even have to look. They would find him.

For some people, entering a couple relationship will give them the most impactful lessons for their individual growth. Some need to learn how to manifest a well-functioning, beneficial relationship. Some simply need the benefits of a relationship. Other people need to develop their aloneness and focus on their internal progress. It depends on what people need the most at their particular stage of development, and it also depends on karmic timing. All situations have their joys and challenges, and all can be used for our growth. What is best and when it is best requires intuition, trust, and courage.

"Let's see if we keep randomly bumping into each other," said Tye lightheartedly. "If we do, we'll take it as a sign."

BACK TO OUR ROOTS

CHAPTER 38

MELT

"You don't sound so good," said Maliyan, answering the phone.

"No, I'm not," said Bell. "I've been sick for a week and can't shake it. My head is in a lot of pain. Can you do something?"

"Yes," said Maliyan. "Are you somewhere you can lie down? Can you put the phone on speaker without anyone else hearing?"

"I'm at home," said Bell. "I'll close the bedroom door."

* * *

"Lie down, close your eyes, and breathe in," said Maliyan calmly. "Hold your breath. Breathe out. Do this again three times slowly.

Rest your arms beside your body, palms facing down. Breathe in and then pat the bed several times with your palms as you breathe out. Repeat two more times.

Turn your palms to face upward. Put your attention on your right palm and feel a ball of energy in it. The energy ball is growing to a couple of inches. Keep your attention there for about thirty seconds.

Move your attention to your left palm and feel a ball of energy in it. Feel the energy growing. Keep your attention there for about thirty seconds.

Move your attention to your third eye, the middle of your forehead, between your eyebrows. Feel that my thumb is pressing lightly on your third eye. It is slowly, very slowly, opening. You can see a tiny ball of light growing to a few inches.

Focus your attention on your right palm again, then on your left palm, and then on your third eye. You're making a triangle. Do it again: right palm, left palm, third eye. Keep going for thirty seconds.

This time, as you do it, move the triangle out to one foot from your body. Right palm, one foot out. Left palm, one foot out. Third eye, one foot out. Trace the triangle in your mind—right palm, left palm, third eye, one foot out from your body.

Push the triangle out to ten feet from your body. Ten feet from your right palm. Ten feet from your left palm. Ten feet from your third eye. You are making a large triangle of energy, and you are in the middle of it. It's a temple. You are the centrepoint of the temple. You are utterly, entirely safe.

Push the triangle out to one hundred feet from your body. One hundred feet from your right palm. One hundred feet from your left palm. One hundred feet from your third eye. It's a large, energetic triangle. All of it is safe. It is energised. You are in the middle of it.

In this safe space, your body and mind expand. Your feet melt into the bed. Your calves melt into the bed. Your thighs melt. Your stomach, hips, and buttocks melt. Your chest, back, and shoulders melt into the bed, to the floor, through the Earth, and into the ether. Your neck melts, and your head becomes lighter and lighter.

Put your attention on your jaw and invite it to relax. Focus on your thyroid at the bottom and front of your neck. It's like a butterfly. It spreads its wings and becomes lighter.

Feel my finger on your left temple. All the muscles and cells in your left temple are relaxing. Then, feel my finger on your right temple. All the muscles and cells in your right temple are relaxing.

In this sacred temple, crystal water runs through the entire space. It runs through you. The cleansing water enters your third eye, moves to the left temple and clears away the blockages and stuck points on the left side of your face. It now moves to your right temple, clearing away all the blockages. The healing water is running behind the back of your eyes, making your eyes feel clean and light.

The crystal water moves to the top of your head, to your crown, forming a ball of energy, and then moves itself in a swirling circle. It moves a foot above your head and makes an infinity sign (a figure eight on its side).

Now, it comes back to your crown and slowly, very slowly, like honey, starts running down the back of your head. As it travels down, it relaxes every muscle and every cell. It gets to the base of your head, where your skull meets your neck, and stays there. It forms a round ball and moves around, clearing the energy.

Your body is completely relaxed. There is space inside. Your mind has expanded into the one hundred feet of the sacred temple. Your body has become loose and light, and your mind has become spacious and translucent."

CHAPTER 39

RETURN OF THE DREAM HOME

Maliyan then took Bell to a new, ever-so-old place.

"We are now going to a faraway place," continued Maliyan. "It's *very* far away, but we'll get there instantly. You'll recognise it as another home, more of a home than where you are now on Earth. You are delighted to be there amongst the majestic trees. The atmosphere pulses with invigorating aliveness. You're standing outside your home, which looks similar to everyone else's home, green and natural-looking. It's a simple home, but it has everything you need. It feels incredibly comforting.

One of the planet's Wise Ones is there to greet you and says, *'Going to Earth is a tumultuous experience, and you must be careful not to start disintegrating like Earth people do. You are safe and can have a pain-free existence.*

*Although you will experience Earth emotions, you do not
have to take them into your body, mind, and energy field.'*

Walk into your garden and see the delightful
flowers and healthy, abundant food that is specifi-
cally synced with you. Sit cross-legged on the soil.
It feels warm, soft, and damp. Take your right hand
and make a hole in the soil. Touch the roots.
Underneath everyone's plot of land is an extensive,
complex, intelligent root system. This system not
only keeps each home's garden alive but is
connected to each person's energy field. The root
system keeps the home occupier functioning in a
vibrant, energised form. Now, dig into the soil with
your left hand. Dig deeper so that you have more
contact with the roots. The root system transfers
its healing energy to you. It feels balanced and
harmonious. It removes the waste products from
your energy field.

The Wise One tells you it is time to return to
Earth. They take hold of your hand and pull you
towards them. As an energetic being, the Wise One
can take any physical form they want. They put
your head on their chest and cradle it.

'You are well,' says the Wise One, reassuringly. *'When
you go back to Earth, take your true essence with you. Your
light does more than you realise. It is helping to elevate the
planet's collective consciousness so that Earth-dwellers
become a more advanced civilisation of beings.'*

Return to your Earth-body. You are pain-free and

happy. Feel the creative fire inside you. Know that any negative experience is temporary and can be healed by remembering who you are. The vast energy system cleans and helps you. It reminds you of your immense connectedness with the Universe."

WISE WORDS

CHAPTER 40

SMALL DEATH, BIG LIFE

One last catch-up tomorrow in Sonder before I leave?

MALIYAN

Sure. C u tomorrow.

◈

The next day, in Black Forest:

As Maliyan weaved her way through the miniature Christmas trees of Black Forest, she pulled a leafy twig from a gum tree and used it to brush away the flies. It was the common bushman's fly-fan.

Turning left, she stopped at Robert's cottage in the side street. She hadn't seen him since last summer solstice. Apparently, not long after Maliyan met Master Xiao, the master returned to China and died a week later. Robert and his wife immediately left for the monastery in the remote mountains of Hunan province. Maliyan assumed they had been there all year because every time she passed the cottage, it looked locked and lifeless.

At that moment, Robert walked out with an A-board.

FREE

Summer Solstice Empowerment

QiGong

All welcome

When he saw Maliyan, he put the board down, bowed, and smiled warmly.

"You're back!" said Maliyan.

"Just back," said Robert. "I thought I better remind people that summer solstice is coming up."

"How was everything in the mountain monastery?" asked Maliyan.

"At the beginning of the year, the morning of Chinese New Year, Master was found on his bed, sitting in lotus position, with a smile and eyes closed," said Robert. "He was dead. By the time we got there, he had already been gone for four days, but his body didn't smell. It didn't smell for the whole week leading up to the traditional barrel burial. Although most people are cremated so they do not hang around their bodies, enlightened people can be buried because they know what they are doing when it comes to death."

Someone in a passing car honked their horn and waved at Robert, who waved back.

"We then helped the ten remaining monks with the monastery," continued Robert. "They are all in their eighties and consider me a youngster. They couldn't cope with the workload of the monastery, so my wife and I arranged for tradespeople to come. We also tended to their personal needs. It took six months to sort out the monastery and aged care visits. At that point, my wife left to visit family, and I stayed behind to redo a one-hundred-day fast."

"One hundred days?!" said Maliyan.

"Yes," said Robert. "When I was fifteen, I visited Master Xiao in his mountain monastery and expected a wonderful summer holiday. After a few days, Master told me I was ready for Biguan practice, a one-hundred-day fast in a dark stone chamber. It's obviously a very demanding practice, but Master was never wrong about such things.

The chamber was behind a camouflaged door at the back of the main temple. We walked through the narrow corridor, down, down, down, deep beneath the temple. We reached another door. Inside was a small room made of granite slab. There was a water jug, bowl of rice, toilet bucket, simple bed with a straw mattress and woollen blanket, and a meditation cushion. Master gave me instructions and left me a lighted sandalwood incense stick. He visited every day and lit another incense stick.

I was given a tiny amount of food for the first twenty days. Every time Master visited, he empowered me with his touch. After a while, I felt that my body had become a pure point of awareness, and I only used it when I needed to move. Otherwise, to me, it had disappeared.

After twenty days, I was given no more food but had water. Master continued to empower many different energy points in me. A lot of unusual and intense experiences happened. One was the ability to float out of the dark chamber, above the temple, to many different places.

At fifty days, Master taught me a new practice of gathering the world's evils. It is a dangerous practice that must only be attempted under strict conditions. Everything had to be confronted, absorbed and dismantled. Challenging, indeed. My experience went from bliss to terror. As each challenge was met, my blissful state would return in greater proportions. The process is called, in translation, *Small Death, Big Life*. For the final eight days of this process, my master stayed by my side, but I was unaware of that at the time.

Eighty days had passed, and it was time to slowly return to the physical world. I started drinking small amounts of sweetened rice milk, then fruit, then vegetables. There were more lighted incense sticks to help my eyes adjust to light. Master stayed in the chamber for longer periods and talked about minor matters to connect me with the world again. The day came to leave, and we walked out together."

"That's incredible," said Maliyan. "So, you redid the one-hundred-day fast? Who looked after you this time."

"Master Xiao," said Robert quietly.

"I see," said Maliyan, who knew that Robert's master would not have left his side.

"And one of the other monks brought me what was physically needed," said Robert, "which was not much."

"I have to go now," said Maliyan, "to meet my friend in Sonder. It's marvellous to have you back. Your house has gone from locked and lifeless to brimming with unlocked life again."

Robert bowed and said, "I am in Qi. Qi is in me."*

---

* The story of Robert is based on the real-life Robert Peng. However, some aspects have been altered and added for the Nanima Series.

CHAPTER 41

MISS MARPLE

Deciding to leave Sonder's outside area to the flies, Maliyan went inside. Leteisha and her boyfriend smiled as they held the door open for her and then exited. It was Maliyan's first visit back to Sonder since her move to The Flat, and she people-watched.

I'm like Miss Marple, thought Maliyan humorously.

Miss Marple, from Agatha Christie's detective series, was an older amateur detective (unpaid and often unthanked) who lived in the quaint English village of St. Mary Mead. The village's tearoom was the main gathering place of the rural community, and it was a constant source of useful, inadvertent information for Miss Marple. She was an unlikely detective with her kind, somewhat dithery way, leading her suspects to underestimate her. However, her understanding of human nature was super sharp, and her powers of observation were keen. Her invisibility and preference for blending into the background, combined with her intelligence, solved many a crime. Miss Marple said of herself:

"Really, I have no gifts—no gifts at all—except perhaps a certain knowledge of human nature. Human nature is much the same everywhere, and, of course, one has the opportunity of seeing it at close quarters in a village like this."

— MISS MARPLE (AGATHA CHRISTIE)

WORST FEARS AND BEST DREAMS

"Surely, I will find what I want soon," said Luna. "I keep looking."

"You're not going to find it," said Maliyan.

"That's very pessimistic," said Luna.

Maliyan laughed and said, "You are looking everywhere but in the right place."

Luna rolled his eyes and looked out the window.

"Did you put your back gate in?" asked Luna, changing the subject.

Maliyan treated the council-owned and mowed paddock behind her house as her own backyard. Not only could she look out her windows and watch it spread down to the creek, but she also had many animal visitors because of it. The only problem was that there was no gate. Every time she stood at her fence, her spirit would bound over to the green beyond, but her body got stuck behind the fence. Thus, she asked the owners if she could put a gate in. No skin off their nose.

"You wouldn't believe it," said Maliyan, "but they said no!"

"They must be worried about security," said Luna. "The trouble is when you lock everyone out, you also lock yourself in."

Maliyan smiled in acknowledgement of Luna's wise words.

"Get an above-ground pool ladder and use it as a stile," he suggested.

Encouraged by his own wise words and practical advice, he ventured back to his problem and said, "Where then? Where is the right place to look?"

"Inside," said Maliyan.

She knew she had to be succinct. She probably had two sentences before Luna would switch off.

"I'm not saying you shouldn't leave," said Maliyan, "but wherever you are, unless you journey within, none of it will work."

One sentence down. Still listening.

"You probably think that if you travel inwards, it will confirm your worst fears, and then there will be no hope."

"What fears?" asked Luna cautiously.

"Everything you think you are," said Maliyan. "I can assure you you are not your worst fears. You are more than your best dreams, but you must discover that for yourself."

LIGHTING UP

CHAPTER 43

BIT OF LIGHT

In The Flat:

Last week, Maliyan took the dormant Christmas box from her garage, pulled out the old, single-thread of LED lights, and wound it around the back fence. In the city, it had always looked a meagre light display compared to other houses. However, it unfailingly made its annual trip from dusty box to fence because a simple hello can be as good as throwing a grand party.

Here, in The Flat, Maliyan was surprised that when 9:00 p.m. hit on the first night of the lights being up, they lit up the surrounding paddock and valley with enthusiasm, turning to outright brilliance as the night progressed. The paddock was dark. The creek below was dark. The farm hill opposite was dark. There were no street lights to be seen, and the lights of the neighbouring houses weren't visible from her fence. In all that darkness, the little lights were having a ball.

When it's dark, thought Maliyan, *you don't need a stadium of lights to make a difference. You just need a bit. A bit of light is a powerful thing when all around is lightless.*

The following evening, as Maliyan checked on her blinking lights, she saw that the farmhouse across the valley now had a row of blue lights on its fence. The farmhouse lights and Maliyan's lights seemed to be winking at each other, tentatively flirting. After a while, they got in sync and pulsed their bright togetherness across the valley and into the town, singing:

> Christmas is coming.
> It's a homecoming.
>
> Forget about your worries
> and all of your hurries.
>
> Together, we are bright.
> As one, we are Light.

CHAPTER 44

WATER AND WEED

After scaling her stile (pool ladder) into the back paddock, Maliyan scanned her newly planted garden bed. When she arrived at the rental, there was no difference between the back lawn and the large garden bed. The whole thing was overrun with Kikuyu grass. You couldn't see where the lawn ended and the garden bed started. The only distinguishing feature was a few tough surviving plants with triumphant flowers amongst the long grass in the garden bed.

It's an art as much as a science to weed old, overgrown garden beds. If you poison everything, then you poison everything! Quick, but deadly. However, you will struggle if you try to pull out all the unwanted grass by hand. From decades of neglect, aggressive grass runners become a jungle of undergrowth, grabbing onto everything and becoming an impenetrable mat. Your weeding will simply be a light prune to which the runners will respond with vigorous, renewed growth. What to do?

You have to be patient and selective. Maliyan did a bit of careful poisoning to infiltrate the conglomeration of entwined runners. Some she shovelled out, which is hard physical work. There was lots of watering to soften the soil, so the runners were more responsive to being removed. And there was careful weeding around the surviving plants, which had to be pruned so that she could see what was happening with them. After beginning the planting process, every evening became a ritual of *water and weed*. Water because new plants are not resilient, and weed because old weeds are.

All in all, it's how we should approach people who need help—tact, perseverance, repeat calm handling, and the occasional deadly word or two to eliminate fatal tendencies. You have to work with them. If you blanket-kill everything that is hurting them, they will collapse under the weight of it and run away. Now and again, something needs to be killed quickly. The root cause has to be eliminated. But most of the time, it's the patient weeding out of thoughts that are not beneficial to their well-being. And you must look for the good and wonderful expression already in them and encourage it to grow. It needs room so that it doesn't have to keep fighting all the weeds of thoughts. It takes time, patience, and love.

CHAPTER 45

LIFE KNOWS

As Maliyan ambled through the paddock, she passed the aged care centre and waved at the ninety-four-year-old man pottering amongst his plants. He was the supplier of the plants she put in her garden. He grew various seedlings on his small allotment and gave them to the Country Women's Opportunity Shop next door. They gave the profit straight back to the aged care centre. The Op Shop was in the original rural hospital. The building was about the size of a large house, tiny by hospital standards, but it would have been a lifesaver to many farmers and their families before the freeway made city access viable.

The plants were on the back steps of the Op Shop, and Maliyan scanned them every morning, well before the shop's opening hours, to see if she wanted any additions to her garden. Not only were the plants dirt-cheap, but they were also grown with knowledge and care. Further, they were entirely acclimatised to the area, which is important for plants. It's no good being a northern city garden when you are a southern country one in the ranges. You have to be who you are. Then you won't struggle. In the same way that we should try to eat what is local, we should grow plants that thrive in our locality. When we are in sync with our particular physical environment, it helps us to flourish.

Maliyan returned to the Op Shop later in the day to pay for her "stolen" plants.

"Thank you so much for coming back," one of the friendly country women said.

Maliyan smiled as if to say, *Of course!* She found it amusing that they usually seemed a little surprised she would bother to come back and pay a few dollars for a plant already in her possession.

They might not know I took the plant, thought Maliyan, *but life does.*

No action is unseen.
No word is unheard.
No thought is unnoticed.

No aspiration is unknown.
No kindness is unrecognised.
No progress is unrewarded.

FIREWORKS

CHAPTER 46

FLAT FESTIVAL

December 21st:

It was summer solstice, the maximum tilt of Earth towards the sun. There were still two months of summer's heat ahead, but deep within the Earth and out into its spacious atmosphere, the turning point had been reached.

Although The Flat was in the ranges like Black Forest, it had significantly warmer temperatures than Black Forest because it was not as high above sea level. Once, Luna said it should be hotter if you were higher because you were closer to the sun. Maliyan wasn't sure if he was joking or not.

It was also the evening of The Flat Festival. When a large planned event happens in a country town, everyone goes. In the city, people often feel lonely amongst so many people, but country towns, being more codependent, tend to be more connected. In Yan Yan Gurt (the tiny town twenty minutes out of Nanima where Maliyan's family came from), events in the town hall were terrific fun. Town life was spun around the regular bush dances, balls, New

Year's Eve parties, birthdays, twenty-firsts, weddings, christenings, wedding anniversaries, and various other landmark occasions.

The 6:00 p.m. festival parade was about to start. It seemed that half the population was on the sidewalk cheering and waving at their friends, and half were in the actual parade. If you wanted to be in the parade, you could practically step into it, walk along, and start waving to people. There was the scout group, the kinder group, the high school drama group, the high school science group, the aged care residents (dressed up and waving through their van windows), the callisthenics group, the highland dancers, the pipe band (with bagpipes), various charities and community advancement groups, and the Fire Brigade. The groups were interspersed with highlights such as a Chinese dragon, a lady on stilts, antique farm equipment, a monster truck, and a lollie-throwing Santa.

As Maliyan had already been at the festival for quite a while, she decided to walk home before the climatic fireworks. She knew she could see them from her back fence. Once home and sitting outside, she became immersed in the sensation of the falling dusk on the excited town and felt herself being drawn to her dream home.

CHAPTER 47
EARTH-WORKS

Dream Planet:

Maliyan did not go to her residence but to one of the regular meetings that the "parents" or Wise Ones scheduled. This particular meeting was called Earth-Works and was for those who lived on Earth.

"Every night, when you sleep on Earth," said one of the Wise Ones, "you are reconstructing the **reality** you experience in your day-to-day life there. Of course, this concept is incomprehensible to humans who believe their physical existence is innately concrete. Regardless of their beliefs, it is not. It is reconstructed every night so that it will seem a certain way on waking. It is done with their willing cooperation, but most are 100% unaware of this arrangement.

This phenomenon explains why sleep is so high on the list of needs for human survival. First is air, then water, then sleep, then food. This may seem surprising. However, sleep-deprived humans lose their ability to reconstruct a strong physical presence. If they are sleep-deprived for too long, their connection to the material experience of Earth will start dismantling, and they will die of some related physical problem.

Once this idea vaguely crosses the mind of a human, a new dimension will open. If reality is unconsciously constructed every night during sleep, then it can be consciously constructed in a more beneficial and enjoyable way."

AFTER A PAUSE, THE OTHER WISE ONE SPOKE.

"The construction of reality leads to our second point for this meeting, which is the concurrent existence of many **simultaneous realities**. There is not only one reality. There are many, and people (and other types of beings) constantly move between them. Although this is pie-in-the-sky to most humans, they can glimpse it by noting how different their reality looks and feels depending on their mental space. One day, for example, everyone smiles at them and plays into their hands like putty; the next, people insult and abuse them. It is not that it just *seems* different. It is, in fact, a different, concurrent, parallel reality.

Can you see how liberating this is? If you do not like your reality, you can shift to one where things work differently. If you are suffering in one reality, you can move to a better one. It is not even that difficult to do. Firstly, the improved version of reality must be pictured very clearly in your mind. What cannot be conceived cannot be born. Secondly, it must be frequently visited until it no longer seems improbable. It must become familiar and a definite possibility. Gradually, it will move from improbable to possible to likely to inevitable."

Swapping back to the first Wise One, the Earth-Works meeting continued.

"Furthermore, as you know, people on Earth see **time** as linear—past, present, and future. It is not. This can be understood alongside the previous two topics. When it is understood that reality is constructed and that there is more than one reality, the concept of time becomes loose. If one can move between realities, one can move backwards and forwards as well.

While we are not encouraging you to explain the concept of timelessness to humans directly, it helps them to move in that direction when they examine something that has healed in their lives. When something truly gets healed, the past can appear to change. This has happened to many people on Earth. At some point in their life, they will understand why someone did something negative (most commonly, it is an understanding of the other person's suffering), and a moment of authentic forgiveness will automatically spring up. Often, after a while, they will look back and can barely remember what used to irritate and upset them so much. The "reality" of the past has unbound itself, sometimes altering the memory, sometimes wholly wiping out the memory.

What is more, some individuals who used to be a large part of their life will tend to "disappear" from their experience (because they don't energetically belong in the new reality), and others will become more present (because their vibration is more in sync with the new reality).

A different experience of life creates not only a different future but also a different past."

IN FINISHING THE MEETING, BOTH THE WISE ONES SAID in perfect unison,

"On Earth, Christmas is approaching. For many people, it is a time of healing and forgiveness because the individual they call Yeshua or Jesus embodies those qualities in a powerful, energetic form. Although the souls of humans always live in the domain of spirit, they are having a 'dream' that they are on Earth, a dream that they must reinvent each night. Help them to make it a happy dream. It must first become a happy dream before the dream untangles itself and reality dawns in stunning light."

WITH THAT, MALIYAN WAS BROUGHT BACK TO HER garden with the bang and fizz of the festival fireworks.

Help them to make it a happy dream, she repeated in her mind as the swish and spark of banging colour lit up The Flat's darkened sky.

STRANGE AND STRANGER

CHAPTER 48

SPIRITUAL STILE

Christmas Day:

TEXT MESSAGE FROM LUNA

Merry Christmas, mi amor.

MALIYAN

You got there safely?

LUNA

Yes, I'm safe.

MALIYAN

Happy Christmas x

LUNA

Sometimes, I wonder why we are friends.

MALIYAN

LUNA

I mean you are not like my other friends.

MALIYAN

What are your other friends like?

LUNA

It's just that I wonder what we have in common.

IF YOU WANT TO FEEL COMFORTABLE, PICK FRIENDS WHO support your established identity. That is okay. It is a sensible life arrangement. However, if you want to grow, at least let one person be a challenge. They may not challenge you in words, but their very existence will challenge the structure of your mind. It is uncomfortable, but if it is someone for you, then you won't be able to untangle yourself from them. You will try. It won't work. You will try to fit them into the life you already have. It won't work. It may be unsettling, but you have found someone who is a spiritual stile, an energetic pathway, to your higher self. Don't waste the opportunity. And if you do, don't waste it when it swings your way again.

MALIYAN

Life, Luna. We have LIFE in common.

CHAPTER 49

TRY AGAIN

As he had told Maliyan, Luna was safe. But he wasn't up north. He was still in the southern city near The Flat. He didn't want to tell her yet. The Christmas holidays became a time of introspection. As he lived by himself, he normally had quite a lot of time alone, but he wasn't usually introspective. He was extrospective. He focused on things outside himself. Generally, distractions. If he felt up to socialising, it was other people. Otherwise, it was T.V., books, and watching sports.

He wasn't entirely sure how safe he was in the internal world. It had always seemed murky, confusing, and disconcerting to him. It made him fidgety and compulsive. Nevertheless, something inside him said that it was time, time to journey inward, and that delaying it would only bring suffering, worse suffering. These were strange ideas for Luna, but they didn't feel quite as strange as they used to. The possibility that he could not feel such a stranger in the strange internal world began to emerge.

He had moments of panic, even terror, in his travels, but a voice (someone's voice, he knew not whose) told him that when the fear is at its worst, when it starts throwing bombs at you and conducts a large orchestra with symphonic madness, then it is close to its breaking point. It told him that if he marched through the moments of madness and terror, they would give in and dissolve under the pressure.

When you are closest to making a breakthrough in your personal growth, your fear throws up the greatest intensity. It will do whatever it can to deter you from moving ahead. If you succumb to its frightening and treacherous threats, pick yourself up and try again. If you forget what you are trying to do, try again. If you change your mind and head the other way, try again. With perseverance, your fear will exit the scene, and you will be standing in a new world.

North or south wouldn't make any difference to Luna, but the choice between out and in would be transforming. Instead of the dreaded inner world being the death of him, it could become the death of his relentless, ever-altering fears and the birth of ever-multiplying improvement and peace. A happy death, indeed.

CHAPTER 50

RUNNING WITH THE RIVER

"I've been much better since we talked last," said Bell on the phone.

"You sound much better," said Maliyan.

"What was that place?" asked Bell. "The place you took me to in the meditation."

"Did it seem familiar?" asked Maliyan.

"Yes and no," said Bell.

"Not long after I moved south," said Maliyan, "I drove to the top of Geboor. As I looked down to Black Forest in one direction and the city in the opposite direction, I heard more of the poem that Francis originally read us in the Nanima poustinia. It went like this:

Look at the town below.
It is you.
Look at the city in the distance.
It is you.
Every rumbling car and pacing person
is you.
Every running child and wagging dog
is you.
Look to the far reaches of the ranges.
It is you.
Look to the endless sky.
It is you."

"When you still lived in Nanima," interrupted Bell, "you took some earth from the banks of the Bell, mixed it into a paste with the river's water, put it on your thumb, drew a line down my forehead, and said, 'I name you Bell-Bell. You run with this river.' Do you remember that?"

"Of course," said Maliyan.

"And, in the very same spot, a year-and-a-half later," continued Bell, "on the last day of my retreat with Euroka, he said, 'When you sit with the river long enough—not sleeping, not making things up, just sitting, just being—there is a chance of becoming, a chance of becoming something more until, one day, you become the river.'"

"Yes?" said Maliyan.

"So, am I the river yet?" asked Bell.

Maliyan laughed and said, "You are the town below, the far city, the rumbling car, pacing person, running child, wagging dog, the far reaches of the ranges, the endless sky, and yes, Bell, you are the river. It is you."

As the energy of the Bell River and the thread of Geboor became more a part of Bell, she became less a part of herself (the fabricated, fearful self). Life passionately longs to dissolve that self and is so utterly selfish that it wants absolute possession.

It is you.
It is you.
It is you.

The End

SUMMARY OF NANIMA SERIES

*A contemplative journey of **spiritual evolution, soulful relationships, and the quiet healing power of nature.***

Spanning four deeply personal and spiritually rich books—**Nanima**, **Geboor**, **Sonder**, and **The Flat**—this series follows Maliyan, an insightful and grounded seeker whose path unfolds across the quiet towns and wild landscapes of rural Australia.

Through shifting relationships, ancestral stirrings, and encounters with both seen and unseen guides, Maliyan's life becomes a mirror for our own inner transformation. Alongside her are Luna—intuitive, witty, and playfully avoidant as he learns to love truly—and Bell-Bell, whose brilliance and volatility reflect the challenges of change and the yearning for wholeness.

The *Nanima Series* offers not just a story, but a spiritual companion. It invites you to walk the path of growth gently, to listen deeply to the land and your own spirit, and to remember that evolution is both quiet and profound.

ABOUT THE AUTHOR

In Wellington, Australia, the rural town on which Nanima is based.

Donna Goddard is a spiritual author whose work blends clarity, devotion, and metaphysical insight. With more than twenty published books across spiritual nonfiction, fiction, poetry, and children's literature, she writes to uplift consciousness and offer healing through words.

Donna's Facebook author page has over 400,000 followers from around the world, and her YouTube channel has received more than three million views. Her books are read by spiritual seekers globally and are known for their honesty, poetic style, and transformative energy.

Her writing is an offering—to help others awaken their own inner spirit, trust its guidance, and create a life of depth, beauty, and quiet joy.

All links at https://linktr.ee/donnagoddard

RATINGS AND REVIEWS

Donna would be most grateful for any ratings or reviews.

ALSO BY DONNA GODDARD

Fiction

Waldmeer Series: A Spiritual Fiction Series
Nanima Series: Spiritual Fiction
Riverland Series (children's fiction 6 to 9 years)
The Fox Tales (children's fiction 8 to 12 years)

Nonfiction

Love and Devotion Series
Sweet Spirit Series
Dance: A Spiritual Affair
Writing: A Spiritual Voice
Strange Words: Poems and Prayers
Love's Longing
Master of Me: Meditations

www.ingramcontent.com/pod-product-compliance
Lightning Source LLC
Chambersburg PA
CBHW020522120726
47904CB00003B/937